Thanks to Ben and Eleanor

Hit For The Hills

Part 1 - Chapter 1

It was a desolate day, dreary and cold, like a morning without coffee. What I was looking at was a Cadillac. Viridian shone on my Elvis belt buckle. December. Some months, the shine was flossy pink. Ellis had pulled up five minutes ago with his dame Berry – clothed in grass green dress, and him; his flannel.

The trip was set, arranged at sunset the prior day. We had arranged to go into town away from all the ruckus my mum was causing me about my job, that being that I didn't have one. Regardless the joints were in the car and ready to be toked like a passing by swallow.

"Get in the ride. We got the sun to follow today," Berry yelled over the sound of the engines tune.

"Straight away," Ellis insisted.

I pulled my skinny black jeans up as if to yell at

them (my head still wasted from the previous night with the two).

Slamming the door shut we ignited in similar smiles towards the weather.

"'Tis a nice day to day," Ellis said. The most to be known of Ellis was his wink and who he gave it to, and that was Berry. He owned a regular loft apartment in town financed by his Fathers will and testament. His Father had been an oil merchant somewhere in Asia. Never saying where to avoid scandal. The death hit Ellis like a hard punch, enough to knock the padding off a loony bin. Life was tough round New Canter – mainly the access to weed and other fine constituents of illegality. But we had made do.

The car was off, starting at a steady speed of forty three, as if we were already on route 66.

Initiating our journey with Sam's. The local convenience store, to buy some more whiskey to warm us up. Berry ran in. Her scarf blowing in the wind…

And at last we started – Ellis and I – perusing the gram biff to the first selection. We did. Sparking the one Ellis claimed, "tastes of strawberries." Picking out the strawberry wrapped jay we sparked up just round the corner as to eliminate suspicion.

"Man, this stuff is heavy, so our day gonna be the same" Ellis stated. "We got a lot of stops before reaching hilltop."

I replied: "heavy is one word, dense is another. Can hardly see the street with this smoke: where else we going?" questioning with a lucid grasp on speech.

"Gimmie a minuet to remember" he coughed (I was beginning to taste the strawberry) when berry wrapped around the corner with tense straight.

"A toke of that?" she asked, with a perked-up smile as if the question was already raised and answered.

"Yeah," we both retorted; it was nice to see her puff like it was nice to eat mangoes. Ellis smirked as if still smoking.

"Don't know what you're smiling for," Berry said. Fortunately for Ellis:
 I did, and smiled the same, to much chuckle.

"Toss that. Its roach." Ellis implored.

She flicked it road wise and into a gutter, an ember flew and my head too.

We struggled getting into the car during such laughter. We couldn't find a reason to not be and that made us more so. It was enough of a struggle; as making crispy bacon. We had smoked too long to escape the crumbly process.

There we sat, through the intersection at Hennigans Point. Town centre. Our heads were dizzy when we parked outside of Cloth Inc., looking to buy a jacket for Berry. The chill had shaken her into wrapping her arms around herself. So we ventured in with yet another joint stashed in my waist coat – Ellis and I looking for the dress room.

Whilst Berry entangled herself in some kind of loopy observation of clothes; we snuck into the dressing room to light my pocket sheathed doobe.

"Quick before someone shows," I lit the silk smooth roll thinking we should probably not be doing what we were. However, we were. So the thought didn't matter. What did was the pass count. We were holding it in to avoid smell detection, 'fire alarms too' we thought as we looked into each other's eyes. The room was smoggy and there was banging at the door.

Part 1 - Chapter 2

We were thrown out by the underwhelming security guard of 5'2 scale. So we abided in the car, lazily listening to the radio of New Canter playing Kansas City; waiting for Berry to get her clothes so we could continue on hollering around.

Berry jumped out the store in a tartan coat green and red lined fitting her dress skirt. She swiftly swung her ass into the car and we began to drive to the cinema.

All three of us excited for the opening of the new film: 'Quest to the Nines; about an alien trapped on Earth with nothing to do, just like us on a sunny Tuesday.

As we entered the cinema, for only 15 bucks, we approached the top row with Berry's legs leading us in to the seats, which Ellis and I were happy about, rather excited in our own ecstatic high still giggling at the store we had been kicked from.

"And stay out," we both quoted the parting words with each other. Sitting down with popcorn and stuffing it.

The film was good, but we were too zapped to tell what happened. Berry told us to stop laughing early on – but the film reminisced of terminator too much so we just laughed at the performance too much.

"Hush up now," advised Berry as we were walking to the doo's she zipped up her new jacket. The nip was on and the sun still high; it was around three o'clock, so we decided to grab a bite to eat at Jerrie's Local grub fatty waffles and coke with coffee.

Entering in supple nature to satisfy an appetite some would call promiscuous – in leu of the cigarette Berry and I had shared, a Marlboro.

Red.

The sit down took strain, especially from Ellis he could smells the pancakes from outside, but once we sat we could bare the smell.

"What're you ordering? Inquired the waitress.

"3 waffles, one with syrup and cream, one with cream, one on its own." Responded Ellis.

"Whose is who's?" I asked.

"Whoever grabs what gets what," he said in glee.

And so, we waited.

"What did you think of the film, Aaron?" Berry turned to me.

"I thought it was a damn good for a sci/fi cash grab." I declared. The table emerged in laughter. As we sipped our water and chuckled still in hold of herbal remedies. At this point we were finding he day ludicrous in nature. All to eventful. But that was our usual cause.

There was a pause between Ellis and I, but we had lost Berry to the mirrors, encaptivated by her troublesome coat, the crimson quaintly sat next to Ellis', hazel eyes. The three of us sat. Impatient. Where were the waffles we wondered in a daint fog of thinking?

As they arrived just moments later, we were puzzled, as we did not realise several moments had past due to the conception of said waffles. Think I had the one with cream.

"Two cups of coffee," shouted Ellis and the waitress was on her way. No waiting around Jcrries, a place for the sane people with only the old ladies to avoid – due to tight regulation of a no complain policy. And there was never a complaint to be had. Needless: the old advocated the place for sanctuary and moaned in other restaurants.

When we left, we could sense there was a roar of relief, we had made some kind of stoned Viking feast of the goods there. With crumbs all over the red and white luxury furniture and clean table.

At one point of the meal we wanted to stay in but thought it pointless. Almost out of money, we hit for the hills, to the top to see sunset with the glimmering of a star bed sat by a great day, as ours was usually inclined to be.

Part 1 - Chapter 3

Ellis thrust the gear into first and off were the wheels to our tremendous day plan.

Going about 60 on the straight way to the busty hills west ward. A conversation started brewing about the day after.
I zoned in halfway through, but definitely heard something on the sexy side about Ellis' sword.

"So, we get up early morn and go to the canteen and drop you off Aaron!"

"Yeah! What you shouting for?" I exclaimed.

"Said that three times damn it. We want another joint. We'll have onc when we post up tree side on the hilltop."

The journey was pleasant, no bickering of any degree; turbulence with the windows was all Berry could muster.

We ended up taking a dirt road up the hilltop parking next to a large cherry tree overlooking the vista; fields of green with trees in view, we all knew it was whiskey hour, and the hour was five.

Sitting huddled round the car interior, we shuffled the botte around, the biff too. Time eventually became skewed and lost to inebriation and inhalation.

As the sun set Berry shifted her head on to Ellis' shoulder. And the panoramic beauty of the suns head fell softly over the distant skies. And, Ellis and I settled to the indefinite future.

There was a scratching at the door of the car round the time the moon rose, Ellis and I had been too out of it to leave the car, presuming it was a racoon or some furry creature of the twilight. With the scrapping stopping in about an hour or so later. We began to rest our heads star ward; to the constellations far away from the light imbued street we called common.

When I awoke, I did so before Ellis and Berry, and was feeling the full effects of a belly lacking sausages and egg.

I lit up a cigarette and stopped outside to hear the wind touch my lips and felt it too.

I could see birds flying south.

Took in the view, some while before Ellis woke up.

"Man, how long you been up?" he asked, blearily.

"'Bout and hour," I replied before he rubbed Berry's face up, rubbing her eyebrows.

"I'm hungry as anything." She spoke languid.

"We'll smoke up and go for a ride back, grab a bite when we swing back home." Ellis offered as the commanding party as owner of the car.

So, we set on down to the canteen; back home. Along the maple tree roads, back to New Canter.

Part 1 - Chapter 4

We stopped in at a roadside canteen for some food. Ordered portions of sausages, bacon, egg, and toast, with all the sugar in our coffees, we still couldn't handle the portions; the whiskey had rendered our stomachs useless, the more we put them to use. Berry was wide awake now, whilst we were still back at the hilltop in our own heads, wasting the night away. Since it was morning and a lovely one. Berry suggested we head past the old park and smoke the rest we had.

Ellis and I agreed, so we flopped down ten on the table with a toss of a few coins and we were off, back to the road we called an escape route.

Having made our way back to New Canter, we hitched up beside Lotterdale Park and strolled through the bark in a blissful state of high ecstasy, our smokes we approved indivisible for any ordinary pedestrian. We posted up by the blossom tree along the trail, letting our hearts see the pink petals fall like a 10kg weight. That's how heavy the sight was. With the sky going grey the two offered to take me back home with my mum. Ellis told me to say, "'you've been at your mates,' she'll smell it on you."

I hoped out the car and slammed past the door just in time for the rainfall.

"Get right here boy! Where have you been? I was worried about you, where were you? You didn't come home for dinner – I baked that stake and you don't even show up! Goddamn it boy. Goddamn." The battle had already commenced with my mum over the semi tenancy; I was away some nights, awake most. The only thing that compelled me was a cig, and I was already enticed.

"I was at a mate's house drinking, Mum." I spoke softly as to not disturb her long script she accumulates.

"If you don't buck up soon, you'll be dead beat and out of time." She revoked pleasantly.

She was a nice enough mum, she only wants the best for me, but my best was a bag of Mary and a black ale. "Won't do me harm smoking, Mum, let me eat that dinner now, huh?" speaking plainly to her as to not start a riot in the house.

"Fine, dig yourself in the dining room for your lunch."

"Okay Mum." I sat down in the dining room table. The chops were in the oven and my appetite for cow was becoming stronger.

"So, who's friends were you at?" She inquired.

"No one in particular."

"Wasn't Ellis' was it?"

"No what makes you think that?"

"The smell of you. Smells like a distillery in here."

"Well I told you I was drinking." I had to twist a lie fast, "playing cards all night." She'd kill me if I said I was out in the cold all night.

"Well stay away from Ellis, you won't get no job with him around – he's never worked a day in his life."

"That's what I like about him," I responded.

"Your stakes nearly ready, would you tell me the truth of where you've been, you seem rough, you haven't been fighting, have you?"

"No Mum; I told you: out at a mate's house. Could I have that stake now? I'm super peckish."

"Oh, alright." Mum said wistfully.

The stake as tough and the sauce sour but made for a lovely lunch.

"Speaking of Ellis, think I'm gonna make my way down to his later on he owes me fifteen bucks." Rather say someone owes me money rather than say I spent it. That way my mum would be more inclined to send me a tenner, seems as if I was being a nice guy, and don't get me wrong. Never had or wanted the opportunity for wrong doings.

"Okay as long as you stay in here for a few hours."

"Okay, Mum. I'll sit a while and read." I slung open my copy of 'Catcher in the Rye' and twiddled my fingers across the pages for a few hours got about halfway through before it shook me that the rain had stopped. So, I slinked on my jacket and made my way out the hefty wooden door.

"Bye mum!" I exhaled.

Part 1 - Chapter 5

The road down was dark, I was shaken. Previous showers had made me cautious; hoping the rain wasn't harbinged by thunder. I scooted my way to town – to Ellis: tried hitching a ride with my thumb to negative avail. I walked with the slightest warmth from my crimson jacket. A red parka. Good for rain but heat not so much.

By the time I got to Ellis' the sky had cleared. Took me a while to get there. My head was booming. The night before had rendered me cognitively useless for another few hours.

My fingers pressed the doorbell and a subtle buzz could be heard.

Berry approached the door; I could hear her whistling. The door opened, she invited me in.

The apartment was a crusty yellow, a 20 deck beside the apples. Pictures of dogs. A dog called

Skippy, and the couple together; Ellis was in the shower, a thing I was looking towards using for the nip.

"Would you like a coffee?" Berry lullabied.

"That would be generous of you, I bet you get it free from work." I humbly reconciled with her.

"You have two sugars and all the milk, I'll run down to the shop now and get some milk. Just wait for Ellis on the settee."

I sat on the black leather couch: to which I had spent many a night on.

Ellis was nine mins and came out wearing silver jeans and a blue shirt.

He sat down too, with both of us exhausted he stuck the radio on. 'Gypsy Eyes' by Hendrix was on, reminded me of a girl from last summer, eyes like sky but shrouded in a dusty turmoil of sexuality. Took a week to get her to admit it, a homosexual I was trying for. Was building up a chance just before she stuck up her shoes for new mud. Somewhere near California, where she could see the sun more often, she supposed.

Ellis and I sat.

"What're we up to tonight Aaron?"

"Nothing much, was grooving on the idea we hit a bar for a dear, play some pool. Mums still against me seeing you, thinks I'm becoming a busted dead beat."

"Only beat you've got is for jazz, Aaron."

"Damn straight." Although I could have agreed with 'dead', (still hungover).

"What a night we had." Ellis stated softly as to not disturb the radio.

"Berry's just gone for some milk; back anytime soon," I imagined. The radio crackled into different stations until we found something snazzy: Ellis was turning the dials.

Glenn Miller popped on and both our hearts fumed with glee.

Berry popped back through the white wooded apartment door and the tree locks chained against each other as she turned the full, locking the door.

"Ellis, dear, are you having some coffee?" she requested, expecting an answer.

"Whatever," he quietly suggested.

She beckoned three mugs, filled the jet-black kettle up with tap water, stuck it on the stove. We all waited, patient. Till I struck up conversation about my fifteen Ellis owed me.

"I'll get it you it back tonight, pay for rounds at the bar later on, Berry check the kettle." He reprimanded.

She did with a Simi vigour vas if to say she knew when it would be ready, on the other hand we could tell she didn't she had started to drift with her eyes closed.

She sprang up and lifted the kettle, poured the water into the mugs full of coffee, then added milk, mine, much. Berry placed two mugs on the table and took hers to the window to peruse knowledge of the climate.

A few hours past as we sat waiting for the sun to fill again.

As soon as it did, we struck off for the nearest gin joint we could find. Berry was reluctant to go; so, she sat solemn in the apartment whilst Ellis and I ventured out.

We parted with the apartment to Flannigens bar. We went inside. The place was jam packet with bikers and lesbians, with one fat guy I knew from the farm. It was a kind of place you look towards when life beats you. Luckily for us that meant: if we smiled, we could get a free shot or two.

Went to the bar ordered two whiskeys, - one dry, one iced – and we sat our jive down next to the bar.

"How's Berry doing?" I inquired

"Proper loose, he replied, "always looking for an excuse to go to sleep, and not in the way I'd like, well at least sometimes, brother."

"So, she's not giving you your special 'desert', is what you mean." I retorted.

"Nothing like that. Think she feels aimless."

"What makes you say that?"

"Like the way she made coffee all puppy like – think she's wondering where time is going.

"Ah, but times goes."

"It does indeed." Ellis finished his whiskey and ordered us two rounds of tequila, (showing such hospitality).

Downed the drink, already fuzzed by the prospect of going home before Ellis demanded we go for a cigarette. The smoke puffed, headlights passed; we went in for another round and a game of pool – Ellis won. And with that I shook his hand, with that, I set off home.

Part 1 - Chapter 6

I kicked my way home, was sober by the time I got there. Mum was in bed, so I snuck in all quiet, grabbed a beer and made camp in my bedroom.

"Where was I last night. Shit. I can't remember. We were out all-night man, if only I could scan my brain for the memory. I'm all fuzzy. Brain done maybe I should fall in bed. Yet this beer had not been drank. Not losing my bubbles for tonight. Hell, I'm gonna do something with myself. Should I get a job and find someplace to live – closer to town. Ellis and berry gonna be tied down some time soon. Damn if that happens before I get my own girl Ellis' is gonna laugh. I mean hell – how am I going to do that. Does it matter? No. I just gotta get my priorities straight and stay away from friends called government. I'd pay my taxes." I thought letting the beer settle. I stayed up most of the night wondering what I was going to do with myself. Wondering if they're be a woman to see next morning. I drifted on that thought as if it were my last, and I swept into a drunken demeanour which pushed me to sleep.

Part 1 - Chapter 7

Awakening on Thursday to the faintest of eyesight; I went to the kitchen for some bacon. "where were you all night, son?"

"Out with Ellis," as I tiredly spoke.

She was often in favour of scolding me on my habits. Drinking, smoking, anything that excused me. We barley talk about my Dad. He had gone a few years back to cancer. Mainly why she wanted me to quit cigs.

I never would though, Dad use to. He was nice and warm. I remember this time when we were playing ball and he had a tremendous fall, breaking his right arm. Was real sore about it. Couldn't go to work for 6 months. So, he was sitting this one time; letting paint dry, with its white going cream – we had painted it together and you know what he said?

"Well at least we ain't dead." Then he got up and took his sling off and walked to the shop. Brought back a quart of whiskey. First time I had a drink, only fourteen. Both of us drunk, seeing the day away.

He was a swell bloke with a lot of credentials: worked at the newspaper depo in town. New Canter Daily. Mainly wrote the crosswords. He was sommat like that. Hooked all the electric in the house himself. He had lived in the house for nearly forty years.

Dad died a month later. Cancer had punched his lungs and he was gone, with a great goodbye, "hit it hard, Kid..." the last speech he had for me. He was always doing speeches; "the traffic," this, the: "Indians" that. "Your mum..." Long winded was his way. Made mine short after he past. Didn't have much to say. A short damask over the damaged emotions.

With only Mum around to pay for things the

house started to fall apart. I didn't have the know how to look after the place; but I would do the cleaning on the occasional.

The day was all sunny. Whipped out a cig on the porch to let the scene take place. Drive by pickups, wanting to see one of those fast rides they make in Europe.

Picked up my guitar for a shanty. Before heading to the shop. Mum wanted some veg and fruit, so I made my way back from the shop. Only took me 10 minutes to get there and back. On the way I saw Mr Peterson.

"How are you doing, Arron? He shouted.

"Fine thanks, and you?" I smeared back.

"just mowing the lawn."

"Nice day for it," I added, "better be any way.

"Sorted," he insisted.

Making my way back I saw a blue jay whistling to its spawn in a tree, cheered me up – jovial.

I got back to the house and rang up Berry.

"Did Ellis get back alright after last night." I said in a concerned fashion.

"Yeah he's alright." She replied.

"Good. Good. Alright. I'll see you later."

"Seee ya!" she awoke the glee in me that permeated from the blue jay before.

Dinner was cooking up and you could smell the stew from the back door. And it was one of those smells that made you wanna sleep. So, I sat up in the dining table with mum and splashed the grub up in no time. Made my way through the pork and carrots with a mean chomp. It was evening.

The road was getting busy, swear I saw Ellis drive by. only made me think of another cig. About three red cars had passed, by the time I had finished. So, I figured I'd go see Dorothy over the road. A little old lady who always had something for me to do.

I walked up to the placid yard lined with red and yellow flowers, (she was proper small about things). Her house filled with nick knacks from the thirties. It was her husband's house who always visits his daughter in Maine. She was a beauty. Always wearing pretty shoes. She would come around once a year for a month, she was 34. I was 19.

Seen her my entire life. Usually visits around summertime.

I strolled up to the door and knocked on the door I had painted bright blue – my favourite colour, it was nice to see when waking up in the morning. Gave me twenty bucks for doing it too.

The door shifted open, and out came the old lady in a knit cardigan.

"Oh, come in young lad before you catch a cold.

I scurried in. her house was all kept tidy, no cats round the place only a small cannery in a wound-up cage. Wings clipped. She let it out.

"How are you my dear," she requested.

"Well I'm still a little wasted from last night, if I'm telling you right." She laughed; she had heard my say that more than once.

"Just came over to see if anything needed doing."

"Well you could sort the dish washer. It won't turn on." She answered.

"I'll give it ago," I said, happy to be of help. I

purposed for a spanner, she obliged.

I could hardly do any handy work. I gave it a bump and turned a few pipes, clicked the switch off and on and it was working again. Then I started it up and began loading her hefty dishes. They were old Chinese ceramic. And, as I finished, she handed me 7 dollars and a cup of herbal tea.

"Blueberry," she offered.

"I suppose why not?" in insisted. She was a peremptory woman. Always on time, tidy, in place. I was all scruffy and always dressed from the day before – which I could briefly remember. Each of us sat in the living room. An old TV with an oak wooden polish besides the elegant fireplace.

"How's Howard?" my curiosity's asked

"Good, he rang me earlier today said he will be

on his way back next Tuesday."

It was Saturday and a long one.

"Would you ask him to bring me a trinket or two?" my room could do with a fresh up."

"Of course, I'll ask him, and he'll see what he can do."

"Well I best be off, it's getting dark. At least it'll be starry tonight."

She escorted me out the house. "My, the tea was lovely. Thank you."

"Not a problem dearie." She waved me off with her problematic smile. I swear she just liked to see my arse around the house. But that didn't bother me. She was nice enough lady.

I waddled along the street vehemently wanting a cig. Pictures of Dorothy's partner and daughter had sent me haywire. She couldn't fly. Her hip was bad.

So, I concluded by sitting on the porch for a cig and watched Dorothy from the window.

I waved back. She fastened the curtains together.

"Mum! I'm back!" I echoed through the house to identify where she was.

"I'm in the bathtub, Hun!" she shouted back."

I lingered through the house reading 'Catcher in the rye'. I liked the ending, made life at 18 seem simple, but after that there's responsibilities. How to pay for bills is a big one. Mum was always struggling for money. Dad hadn't left much, just his shared for New Canter Daily. 15% he owned. Mum and I could live of it just no holidays.

We used to go on them when I was a child. When

I was seven. Dad loved the beech. Me too. When I was ten, we went to see the San Francisco Bridge. At thirteen we went to England to visit the Queen – never met her though. Just saw the palace.

I liked travelling on the planes. Loved seeing the sky from above.

I lit another cig and rang Ellis to see how he was.

He was fine. Told me he had passed by earlier. I knew it was him.

"Was gonna pick you up for a ride. Still wanna go for one, got a little shindig available if you wanna get in some hassle."

"Like what, no fighting right?"

"Nah. You in?"

"Yeah, why not." I responded

"I'll be up there in ten."

"See you," then I threw on my jacket.

Part 1 - Chapter 8

I was waiting for Ellis to turn up when up rocked the Cadillac.

"Jump in!" he demanded. I did so.

"Where we going?" I inquired.

"Racing up Darley."

He revved the engine up and off the smoke went.

"Here have this." He pulled out a white crushed up bag all discreetly as we were cruising up to Darley.

"What is it?" I said, confounded: could have been anything like coke or smack.

"Molly." He said, really, groovy.

"Have you had any?"

"Yeah, I'm gooked!" he exclaimed "Take three big sniffs and rub your gums."

Yet again, I did so.

"It'll take a while to kick in, I'm reaching my peak now, friend."

I sniffed up like a lion's roar, titled my head back and was in a rush for the drop back.

20 mins out from Darley I was beginning to feel timid, "Who'er we racing?"

"Some blokes from up county – cash prize is 300 bucks, killa."

You could tell the molly had hit him hard, his jaw dropped like an in-heat bulldog. And the things he was muttering of the same language.

"Slow down." I said, "feds."

There was a cop car on the other side of the road. He slowed, and they did give us a glance from an awkward distance, they erupted of in high speed, not by the job perspectives.

"Fuck," declared Ellis. "that was close."

"Tell you what's close: this molly. Swear down I can feel like an echo of snow."

"Ha," he proclaimed, "darn right, feels like my skin is a river, and my eyes are of the tiger."

I began to snicker.

"How long till we get there?" I asked.

"Only two mins." Ellis replied

"Good. I'm starting to feel like rocket fuel."

"Good. Good… let the high take hold."

So, I sat back, reclined the seat and strapped my seat belt and looked forward as we approached our opposition.

They were in a rhino red Ford. We skimmed beside them, and Ellis waved to them. It was at a deserted junction. They sent a wave back.

The engines began to rev, I was feeling ecstatic, Ellis swept the gears into a spark and both cars flew off, zipping through the air like a falcon. The ford was still beside us down the strip of road, zooming. Ellis shifted gear; we were falling behind when Ellis slapped into second gear, speeding past the post office. They were gaining speed, but Ellis boosted into third gear and we were winning. Storming through Darley with a tremendous high, endless zest for being fast.

He dared into forth and the ford chased us past the front doors, the engine was firing like a colt 45. when he pushed into fifth roasting the finish line.

We blew up in a stupefying vibrancy.

"Woooo! We went, with a blood rush.

We pulled up to the side of the road, waiting for the Ford to pull up but they went on; still speeding. And they were gone.

"Blast. My 300!" Ellis was vexed, the winners fee was tossed.

"If I ever see that chump fuck; I'll beat him!" he yelled.

"Leave it, we need to crash at yours quick, we must have raised some eyes."

The high was beginning to soar angelically. We were buzzed. Loopy and crazed by the molly. Our eyes glinting with chaos, we ran the car back to town as if we were still racing.

We had begun to calm down, but Ellis remembered his girl and got into rancid excitement.

He flung open the door. The time was 3am and Berry was in the bathroom when she rushed out to meet us.

"We won, baby, we won!"

"Yes! I knew you would, where's the 300?"

"It's gone, the goddamn sleaze bags ran off before paying us." Ellis remarked. "That money was for Aaron."

"It's fine. It's fine. Don't need no money." I humbly added.

"No worries." Stated Ellis.

"Man. This high is kicking." I spoke out.

"No worries, I've got a blunt."

He lit it quick as he could and there was a mist of fog engulfing the apartment – fast. We passed it around a few times before it hit us, we were in a frenzy of exuberant senselessness.

I had fallen asleep on the couch, shuffled next to the couple. I then got up and made a coffee, the kettle didn't disturb the two.

I mixed the coffee and sugar, added milk, took one sip and my eyes began to open.

Figured I'd slip out after my coffee. Let the two settle when they woke up. I left a note and set back off home, leaving just as the sun shone over the buildings adjacent the entrance.

Part 1 - Chapter 9

The home journey was sore. Could hardly stand. Rendered abysmal by the night. My arms not with it and legs aching; I got home to the cold porch. Sat myself down on the rocking chair and sat a while – going back and forth as to ease the notion of physical tension. Water was at my bequest; I was starting out for some when mum popped out with a glass of milk. "Here you go son." She placed the pint in my rusty hands, I guzzled it down softly.

"Where have you Aaron. You can't keep staying out all hours of the night coming home from doing God knows what and turning up like you been in a hell spot."

"I know mum. I'm doing my best here." There was nowhere to work in New Canter, or no jobs to which I felt qualified.

"Well you better not be going out tonight. Okay."

She implored.

"Okay, okay." I whisked her away through the milk drops on my moustache.

She went inside and I was left to the frost bite, waiting for a glistening sun.

"I liked the sun, the way it flows out, how it plays hide and seek with the moon and gets caught out in autumn. If only I had something to do... maybe reach down to the shop for a pizza, hell perhaps another beer to suit this chill; mum said rest though and hell I'm beaten. Last night was power and my throat is still giving me drop backs. Maybe I should just swing on the porch. Back. Forth. All day smoking." I pondered as I moved to grip a Marlboro

I lit my cig and began to feel better, the dense smog.

It was a serene for a Friday (which Fridays are

for). Near the housing that led away from New Canter, call it the suburbs. Unfortunately, there were no girls around for me. Last time I spoke to one; beside Berry; was at the shop. A nice girl. Small and short with black hair and a simple smile, I asked her out, but she said she had no time, was too busy.

So, I concluded it was best not to keep asking. Real pretty though, one of them dames you could see yourself tying with. Always wanted to be with a girl. Had girlfriends when I was sixteen. Holly. Ginger. Freckles and all. She lived in an apartment with her parents, a small crummy place where there was damp – you could tell her farther was hard working: he owned the shop underneath selling gardening tools, irony being the wasn't a plant in her house and absent lawn. She was all puckered up this one time on our third date and I kissed her just as she ate the last of her ice cream. She tasted of vanilla. Then we cascaded with sex, like bulls. She was older than me. 17. She had a curfew, but always came to see me, not exactly legal, but cops in town were lazy, most of them undermining the importance of control. New Canter was relatively safe place, with barely any danger in sight with the, "maybe," from Mum to, avoid back streets near Christmas."

I wasn't excited for Christmas this year. Mum and I couldn't spend much, but I had gone out of my way to buy her a pink hat I had stowed neatly under my bed. Wasn't expecting anything for the effort though. I am an atheist, so the prospect of some fatty sneaking through the house was not the greatest of concepts to me.

I had always been like that: even before Dad had passed – cynical. Always thought the news was rigged like elections. That there must be aliens spying on me. Wacky stuff made sense to me, when you get too far out you start to look in and see the picture. And most people tell the truth my mate once told me he'd seen a werewolf. Could have been a cat scratching himself whilst he was tripping balls on acid, having known the gulf. But there was truth in his eyes I couldn't disregard. Other than the scratch marks on his arm, I didn't have much else to ask.

Funny how people have stories about weird stuff. My life had always been simple. Up for school, up for mum. Hadn't really done too much with my life. I was a real good writer in school but couldn't get a grip on maths very well. Once wrote a story about the undead at the circus. Other than that, only notable thing about school were the fights. I avoided them but Ellis was the one forever in them. Ellis had a mean temper he could be rubbed wrong so easily. Nowadays he keeps things in check, his words sometimes get violent – a kind of passionate frenzy of all too well a comprehension to the meagre of idiocy, often getting mad at people for the stupidest of things. He could not bear stupid people, which I thought sweet. Berry felt as if she were dumb which always lead to the two of them having a cuddle. They were my favourite pair. Didn't really share too many mates that was Ellis deal.

I liked the quiet, but a record, loud, with speakers; I could do.

I lit another cig and sat my eyes towards the inside, after I finished, I went inside and jumped on the couch.

"Mum, will you turn on the radio?"

"No!" She screamed from upstairs.

I slept. Woke up mid-day, feeling comfy I wacked the radio on. Put on Wizz central, looking for some rock. Aerosmith blasted on and I made my self respite on the couch some more.

Part 1 - Chapter 10

Mum was poking me for dinner – a few hours had past, "come on, get up. Pork chops and vegetables.

"Oh alright," I drowsily revoked, with hinged eyes. The smell woke me up. I sat down at the dining table and began chomping my way through the meal.

"Slow down," Mum insisted.

I did. Swallowing was hard after the night before. A difficulty I appeased.

Mum ate quietly as to not disturb the mood. "Are you going out tonight, Aaron?"

"Nope, staying in. the last few nights have tired me. Need my senses back."

We ate.

Part 1 - Chapter 11

I rose from the table and began to wash the ceramic, opened the back door then heard a howl from a dog down the street somewhere. It was half 6.

I took to my bedroom to sleep, wondering, "am I gonna get outta here anytime soon? Never." I wanted to head south to see if the beds were as comfy as mine. But didn't want to leave mum in case her bad hip became active. It was my dream though. The big city with burger stands; a place where I could be free to act and flow without constrictions. It was tight round new canter. No big jobs, those type of deals that make you question why you bought it? My whole life I wanted that massive wad of cash in my back pocket. Only had my miniscule savings, 300, might get me some place.
Bang!
I sprang up jolted outta bed and rang up to the doorstep. Saw Mr Jefferson's door shut with the

radiating glow from inside disappearing. I ran down the raggy road to see, roughly, where the shot came from. Growing breathless just as I saw it.

A rottweiler dead. Shot. Blood smearing down the door stop of Jefferson. I was incredulous. The dog was whelping and crying – the last of his life in my hands. It looked at me began whimpering a sigh I'd rather not hear.

Then he passed.

I stood up.

My eyes beginning to look home wards, to ring the cops. As I got in, I rang 911 to see if they could dispatch someone to clean up the spent hound.

They arrived ten minutes later asking what the problem was.

"A dog has just been shot down the road. Outside Mr Jefferson's."

"We're on it pal."

The three of us lulled down to the body. The first officer was called Terry and the second Clarence.

Terry inspected the body and found a bullet hole close to the abdomen. Clarence stood arriving at the vista for the perp.

I stood lonesome, wondering who had committed this vice, drawing my gaze to Mr Jefferson, who was outside now with most of us on the street.

"Mr Jefferson, what did you see?" Terry asked. Mr Jefferson was also a member of the police force, had been for fifteen years.

"Nothing! Only all you are standing outside my house late at night, caring for some feral thing outside my doorstep." He angrily stated. "come on you all, haven't you ever seen a dead dog.

Someone from the crowd said "no," Mr Jefferson pull a fowl face.

Clarence buttered in, "nothing is wrong everyone, we just want a few names and testimonies."

"Good!" Shouted Mr Jefferson. "Away from my house."

Everyone cleared as Clarence blew a whistle, leaving me with the cops and Mr Jefferson.

"Who do you think did it?" I asked.

"We've got no suspects at the moment." Terry declared, "gonna have to come back tomorrow and ask."

"Take that carcass with you." Snarled Mr Jefferson.

The two loaded it up in their car and went off without a further word to anyway. They didn't care too much. I went back home and told mum what all the ruckus was about.

I knew it was Mr Jefferson. Who else has a gun around with them, a cop.., not even old Phillip the gold miner from the bottom has a fire arm. An inkling of righteousness swept across me. If it was Mr Jefferson, he would need to be exposed. Couldn't do a thing that night, fell on my bed questioning: who was it? Why? The dog was so gentle. Was it the one barking earlier?

The event had shaken me. And still on my comedown; finding sleep difficult. So, I sat on the porch smoking the entire night on the rocking chair and began to drift asleep.

Eyes opening to the post man.

"Hey Aaron, here's your mail."

I took the mail off him, waved him bye and off I went inside, searching for some toast.

Part 1 - Chapter 12

"Who do you think killed that dog?" mum asked

"No idea," I said, even though I had my suspicions of Mr Jefferson's: didn't say to avoid curmudgeons.

"Well whoever it is better fess up soon, so they don't get penalised."

"They'll show up for certain, Mum."

I left her there and headed into town to pick a new vinyl up for the record player. The sky was grey, a Sunday.

The store was bleak, no customers. Meant I could have a decent rummage. Looked at everything from Hendrix to Boston. Picked up a rockabilly record. Tracks from the 50's. shindig action. Cost me three dollars.
Decided to shake Ellis out for a joint, it was our

custom to on a Saturday.

He swooped out the front door fastening his belt, "Hey there killa. How are you doing?" he said joyously.

"Good," I replied, "but Mr Jefferson dog killed a dog last night."

"What?'

"A dog was killed last night, man," the marijuana hit me; I was already feeling more alert and better. "Man, I heard a gunshot and ran my tail down the street, saw this rottweiler dying. Held him in my hands but he passed on. Swear tell you who done it as well: Mr Jefferson."

"The cop?" he asked hushed.

"That's the one, hey keep quiet though."

"What we gonna do about it?"

"We gonna sneak into his house and find the gun he shot it with. He always leaves the back window."

What time?"

"All the time."

We began to realise our capabilities. We weren't cat burglars, but we would sneak out of class enough to know the score. Then we stood, in our hazy daze questions. The smoke was strong, but I couldn't laugh. The previous night had hit me too hard.

Ellis however played a painting of script for the day, planning out what to do.

We drove round most of the day blipped. Listening to radios eating burgers. We ran into Berry at the coffee shop, so we went in and offering our wallet.

"Hey boys!" she exclaimed pleasantly. "What are you having?

"Two coffees, like usual. With two doughnuts." Ellis pursued his mind for a smile to use. What came out was a sorta pinkish towards the waitress. Whilst I was planning to rob the doughnuts.

Putting that aside, the high had caused an appetite massive, and a stance feeble.

We sat.

Berry brought out both of the coffees out with an apron, grabbed a chair besides us and started to natter.

"Hey, did ya know about that shooting last night, near yours Aaron. What happened?"

"Dog was shot." I replied with hesitation.

"What'ye acting like that for." She chuckled

"It died in my hands," I spoke gravely.

Her smile changed into an abysmal silence. "My God are you alright?" she asked.

"Yeah just trying to figure out who did it. Ellis and I are going to go house to house to find out who it was. There's only 8 people on our street and it sure weren't Dorothy.

"Well who was it, I'm dying to know." She said abruptly.

"We don't know for sure, cops couldn't be arsed, but they took the corpse. We gonna swing by and see what the crack is."

"Oh, can I come?" she asked.

"Sure." We both mimicked

"When I clock off work come for me. Be around 4." She cheerfully chirped.

The two of us payed our dues and went back into the car promptly. Took the ride to the car park for a smoke out.

We both swayed in the Cadillac car thinking of muffins and popcorn. Our twain gasping for air through the dense fog we had combusted.

"Do you think we'd catch Mr Jefferson out of it then?" asked Ellis.

"For sure, keeps his gun in the kitchen, went his house when I was a kid. It'll be a wonder if he still keeps it there."

And as we wandered our eyes danced over the varying parked cars to commute and view.

We slicked back for a few hours, messy and in need of Pepsi. We deposited the car in a gas station, filled up the tank with a chipper clicking. There was Maurice, a black man who was indignant towards white folk. He got enough sales and always smiled at me.

I searched about for a cola and: my sight to dazed to navigate I turned down the fresh food isle and began to hear difficult kafuffle from the main desk.

I shadowed round with my cola in grab; it was a robber and was tense enough to be a gym goer.

"Money!" He vehemently demanded.

"Okay, okay." I was in shock before the idea came to me.it was a hard fall and a hard pop. The can exploded: I had hit his head he heckled for a gun when I upper cut him with my right. K.O.

"Thank you" Praised Maurice.

"No problem." I stood elegant. "Let me ring the

cops." I said.

"No bother, get yer self some can, maybe a beer." So, I did, chugging that red ale out of the door.

I smashed in the car and told Ellis of events taken place.

"Dang hot! He exclaimed, ecstatic, "and you got cans too. Darn we having fun."

"That weren't no kind of fun." I said.

"Don't be a downer," Ellis implied. It was still another hour before we could pick up berry. I knew that would go quick. Not as quick as it did.

We trailed up outside the coffee shop with a honk. She pulled open the door with some fire. Shuffling into the back seats all agitated.

"What's up darling?" Ellis asked.

"I broke some plates when I was thinking about that dog, made me damn angry."

"Well calm it down. We got people to see. Gotta make it look like we don't know about Mr Jefferson"

"Alright, alright. I'll cool." Her voice turned husky.

She cooled and we set off. The drive was filled with an eerie silence.

Part 1 - Chapter 13

The car galloped down the road before we hit my house. Berry was already ready to start asking around. I put my record in the house and said hi to mum. Then got back out onto the street with Ellis, Berry had already seen to Dorothy.

"She daint see anything." Berry reported.

"I knew she wouldn't." I said. She skipped to Ellis to finish the inquisition.

First was Mr Thomas, the 22-year-old doctor. The three of us knocked on.

We all initiated at once after the hard knock, it flipped open, "Hey."

"Welcome" He responded. "How are you doing on this fine Sunday?"

"Fine." I replied.

"Look, what're you here for. Got cooking to be doing, can't keep me for long."

"We were wondering if you know who killed that dog last night."

"Oh yeah. The cops were round earlier. Gave me a questioning; to the point: I really don't know. Heard the shot and ran out, saw Aaron holding him." Seemed to me like he was in a hurry. But that's the way things were down at the clinic. Everyone had colds on account of the bitter weather."

Mr Thomas started speaking, "ran out just a few moments after I heard the shot, why you asking me anyhow?"

Ellis butted in before I said anything, "see the cops can't find the killer, and we can't have someone trigger happy walking round Dorothy and Aarons mum."

"Anyhow boys; I'm gonna leave you. Don't know who did it, and if the police don't know who did it, I doubt you three can find out. Goodbye." He closed the door all soft like a cat through the flaps – he was always nice Dr Thomas, not the kind of bloke who could kill.

We marched to the opposite house. It was Carol Hidgings. We were slowly catching round to Mr Jefferson.

We wanted to trail round though to avoid suspicion and find the suspect - maybe off cuff it was someone else.

"Hey Carol.' Berry initiated after a slight press of bell; Carol was there in a hoot.

"Hello young children," she was fifty.

"Hey miss." I spoke.

"Hey darling.' She rushed into speech. She was excitable.

"How are you doing carol?" asked Berry.

"Swell thanks. And you?"

"We're all fine. Look I know you're in a hurry. We were just wondering if you knew anything about that shooting last night." Berry ignited with sheer positivity.

"Well, No." she gist fully responded, "I heard the shot and ran out to see Aaron cupping the poor creature. I waited a holler before going out the door, had to make sure it was okay before I left the house. Not about to hear shooting and go out and run in the direction of it, oh.'

"Are you sure you didn't see anything at all?" I asked plainly – (you could tell we were staying at the front door for too long).

"Nope, nothing at all. Why've you come asking anyhow?"

"Well as you said if there's someone round shooting its best to find out who. At least for the neighbourhood" I released these words carefully.

"Agreed." Carol consummated. "I really must be going, was cooking up a mean chicken in the kitchen, if you hadn't noticed the stench already." She was one to drift on, "well see ya. Hope you find who it was soon- I'd feel safer."

"We will. Don't worry carol." Ellis supported. The door slammed briskly shut like a buttered bee; we were off to the next witness. If we had cookies instead, we would have been killing it with cash, but so far: no one knew anything.

We sauntered down to Mr Peterson next. He was not there when the predicament took place. I knew he wouldn't know anything, he was always too drunk on his own wine; as we approached the tattered green landscape we all butted together in a semi huddle readying for Mr Peterson – our plan not in place and to be abruptly improved. Our haste commenced to the door all three of us ready to confront the ruse.

Ellis had to knock.

He insisted the door to open. we loved Mr Stevenson, on account of him being a drinking buddy, occasionally.

Ellis knocked five times, then I knocked a quick 2, a moment then I knocked quick 2 times. He came to the door – first name: Gary.

"What're you three doing here. Aren't you supposed to be having fun somewhere?" stated Gary. "out there making smell."

"Yeah," Ellis said, "about that...we're here to find out some information on who killed that dog last night."

"Yup that shooting alright, woke me up alright and I was hammered, remember briefly seeing Aaron, just there, at the ordeal, Mr Jefferson and his lawn. Wonder who did it? Spoke to the cops earlier, but I couldn't get a word in hedge wise. Looked like they were in a hurry, probably couldn't be arsed with the situation, if someone's just walking round with a gun you would think it damn important."

"But no – they gotta get their coffees. All the folk round here should be signing off for an officer patrol round here but what we get? Two hustlers trying to walk off the beat. Hurump I say."

"We say the same, but we could catch who did it today I bet." Ellis spoke.

"Well what good are you three gonna do?"

"We've been asking everyone around here for some info, see find out who it be." I answered.

"No wonder you ain't found nothing ain't likely you gonna find much more than your dinners back at home, if you're asking me." Gary said in a golly hip solid sway.

Berry chimed in, "are you sure that you didn't do it, Gary, you're always in a drunken stupor."

"No; I didn't do it. Don't you know I'm vegan? Could hardly touch a pigeon."

"If you say so.' We were three doors down from Mr Jefferson's. berry waved Mr Stevenson and we erupted down the lawn way to Clarence and Peters house. They were a gay couple: to sweet pies from college. They had hooked up and ran away from home to live together, home just being half an hour away. The two ran to the doorway, questions in their eyes.

"Hello Aaron, Ellis, berry. What're you doing knocking on here?" Clarence curiosity inquired.

"Here about last night. Saw Pete last night but not you," I replied briefly.

Clarence started speaking, "We're having a little party to ourselves when the gun shots."

Pete had come down the stairs saying, "yeah I was having a good time with Clarence then got frightened by the noise. Went to grab knife in the kitchen. Awfully scared; Clarence ran out before I could say anything. When he came back and told me what had happened, I was in shock."

'That's why we're here," indicated Ellis, "don't want any one round here to feel unsafe,"

"Good" stated Clarence, "we ain't too fond of that sort of chaos about."

"I ain't either," said I.

"Do you know who could have done I?" berry

interjected.

"No idea. It was outside Mr Jeffersons, maybe ask there." said Pete, worryingly.

"We been down the whole street, and no one's heard a peep, regardless of how the shooting was," Berry indicated.

"If you don't, we ought to be off." Clarence claimed.

"See ya thanks for helping out.," Berry calmed.

The two slid behind the orange shaky door and closed it softly.

We were well on our way to Mr Jefferson's now, of whom Pete seemed suspicious

Jane was next. We kind of had a flirt a while back though the two of us were beyond that. I belted the door with my foot to no avail.

We were kind of on crummy terms on the account of our connection. She still liked me. I just thought there was something off about her that I could not be to bothered to find out – she opened the door with a kind of glee.

"Heya Hun; what're you doing here? Are you hear about that dog?" she screamed all hushed.

"Absolutely," I said, "thought you'd be the person to ask," she was one of those girls that knew the gossip. Always on her phone chatting."

"Well I did see Mr Jefferson out on the yard after a popping sound."

"That's the first time someone has known something" I declared.

"Why who've you asked?"

"Everyone on the street," said Ellis

"You better ben on your way to catching who did it."

"We are." Announced Berry.

The three of us turned with a march when Jane said, "Hey Aaron come down for a fling maybe tomorrow – just knock on and go." I was impatient

"Maybe," I resulted.

"Okay see you then." The door closed.

Part 1 - Chapter 14

The time had come. I fastened my laces proper and headed to Mr Jefferson's, "look," I began to plan: "Berry you knock round front and distract Mr Jefferson. Whilst the two of us will head round back and sneak in the window."

"Alright," replied Berry.

The two of us jumped the creaky fence to the back door, avoiding the nettles at our footing. We hurried to the back door. the dainty window was open.

Ellis boosted me with no words spoken. The kitchen was dark, unsafe, with plugs filled and wires cascading, running along water taps. I was shocked, abysmally chasing sight round in a frantic scurry, I pulled past the door, down the doom corridor; he was wearing his purple dressing gown.

I went for the stash where he hid the gun. I extracted it from the second draw. Whipping out a revolver and steadily throwing the cylinder, checking, 5 bullets. I gaped in awe; I was right. Just as I stuffed the gun in the back of my trousers, Jefferson had spotted me.

I jumped out the back window and landed on Ellis, we both got up in a frenzy.

"Quick let's shift!" I shouted. Ellis led the way and burst through the damaged fence. Berry was at the driveway with Jefferson not in sight.

We all bolted down the street just as Jefferson bound out the house, shotgun in hand, perching on his driveway as we swung past in the Cadillac. Berry flung through the window.

Jefferson shot; hit Ellis in the shoulder. And the wheel span leaving us stranded for control launching into a streetlight.

"Who'd do ya think ya are messing with me?!" Jefferson shouted, "taking my goods."

He fired once more, popping the back-right tyre.

"Berry, stay in the car." I swung out the passenger. Confronted by Mr Jefferson with his aim in play.

"Look we just wanted to know what you were up to."

"Why are you tangling in my affairs, last mistake you made." He went to pull the trigger.

I was quicker. Grabbed the gun from my trousers and shot him dead. His pose stood. Blood threw out his throat, he laid himself on his lawn.

I went to his side. "I didn't mean to do that. If you hadn't had killed that dog this never would have happened." I was near begging for forgiveness when he said:

"Good shot kid," and his eyes fell into a void of sleep. The sun set.

Part 1 - Chapter 15

Ellis awoke three days later. Dr Thomas was attending him when he woke. The police had been fair about the affair. Jane had seen the ordeal and Pete confessed about the dog, leaving the police with us. I was worried about Berry. She had cried all the previous day.

Ellis's' first words were, "where is my coffee."
We all smiled. Happy.

"The shot has punctured your arm but not much more." Dr Thomas announced.

"That IK can feel." He added.

Berry chuckled, "at least the sense of humour is back."

"Damn hurts like hell though."

"It will for another four weeks." Dr Thomas

postulated. "would you like to go home or stay here?"

"I'll stay a few days."

"in that case I'm off," I said, "glad you're okay big boy. I'll visit tomorrow."

Caught the bus back home. Said hi to mum. Put my vinyl on the record player, blasted back on the sofa fatigue man I had killed someone. some fall. Was excused by the police on account of Mr Jefferson going psycho. Could tell from his house that a screw or two went loose. I lit another cig, finished it and stubbed it out on the revolving record.

Part 2 - Chapter 1

A month later and it was snowing. Christmas had past and mother bought me a bottle of bourbon. I gave her the bottle of wine and we both had a drink each.

Cousin Lemy had visited and he brought a smell. He left to go skiing. Sounded exciting.

I was up and ready to the smell of curry and rice from the last night. Mum and I had a feast, she would always pry, ask me if I was alright – after what happened; I always said 'yes' , but there was a burn worse than jack in my stomach, maybe my guts, I didn't know anatomy too well although I knew that type of action would leave you with something and damn did it.

I was staring at the ceiling for a few weeks going over stuff in my head, what difference could have been made that day avoid cosmogenous behaviour. Maybe we should stop snooping around as such, if I only said yes, 'let's go on a holiday' regardless, Ellis said we were gonna go cross country and he would pay.

I'd always wanted to do it. To see the sights across America and I always had time - we were thinking of going when the snow had cleared. New canter looked a nice ice white.

I got up and saw the view from my window; snow covered the lawn and on the streets. I made myself coffee put on my scarf on and sat on the porch and smoked a while, till my drink was done. After I decided to go visit jimmy. An old mate from school. He was Christian. Mass every Sunday the whole shebang.

Was feeling for some comfort. I believed the thing, just knew that company would be swell, and he'd at least make a hot chocolate.

I put on my boots and ploughed through the snow. He lived only three blocks from the away but in the weather, it seemed like five.

When I arrived, Jimmy was shovelling the snow away from the driveway to the garage. He had a green sports car made somewhere in Europe. I wasn't great at cars but knew how fast they could go. I could hardly drive.

I threw a snowball at him.

"Hey Aaron, what you doing that for, don't you know that's water combat if only I had a water gun, you'd be colder than a steak in the freezer."

"Heyo chap!" I shouted from the garden path. "was wondering if we could chat for a while…"

"Sure thing." He offered simply.

We went inside and abided the time by turn on the kettle. "Your parents in work Jim?"

"Yeah should be back around five," it was ten

thirty-two, the kettle hit off and Jim poured us both a hot chocolate then we sat in the front room on the relaxed on black leather sofas.

"What brings you down my way Aaron?" he inquired.

"Well, I think I'm going the right way for a beating soon, meaning I'm not getting along with my mum, smoking too much weed, enthralled in the liquor, and I have to buy a carton of cigs each day. – I don't know ever since – "

"The shooting?"

"Yeah – I don't know what to do with myself." I paused sipping my hot chocolate, "I don't know where I'm going in life, what to do. Was hoping you'd have something to help me with. Like some big speech that would make me do something drastic, like change genders and become a nun, or join the army."

He chuckled with an eminent retort, "maybe you should just go on holiday."

"I'm gonna go cross country as soon as the snow has cleared."

"Good on you, it'll do you some good.' Spoke Jim.

There was a silence as we sat. The past crept in and I thought it best to leave.

Part 2 - Chapter 2

A wink I passed at a mag pie that laughed at the breeze, swept sadness into my eyes, felt like a cold needle

The walk home was seldom, no folk to cheer, nothing to chill the sombre I felt. There was a grassy spot that I trotted on, with cat paws yellow too, I turned the corner, and, at my sight, the beauty was there. That Cadillac that had my stare.

Ellis was sitting on the porch, saw me, and Hollard flashing his dollars.

"Come fly with me." his words hit like a sore fist.

"What you doing?" my curiosity claimed.

His eyes were full of vibrancy, a colour you could see if you were standing straight.

"Picking you up so we can go for some mugs at mine, pass the time and take flight."

"Draw you mean."

"Bought a stack of L&B as much weed as my pockets could carry, hence the cargo shorts."

He passed a 'heh' under his breath. Stood up and gripped the car door.

"I'll come.' his company brews blood, an open view of the day. He drove semi haste towards his place.

"What a hell of a day" he spoke "been awake all-night fulling my lips for Berry's hard kiss."

"She at the flat?" my own lips kinda spat into the wind

He turned his head like a carousel. "she goddamn better be. She's part of the surprise."

"Up darn toootin', throwing suspense every day."

"Are you gonna ask what it is?" he asked in monotone.

"Ether it's a chic, some coke, or you bought a new lamp." a witty answer.

"You got the last two, but it's something fun, settle us down a bit."

"Damn right, push the peddle."

The wheels revolved, shooting of into the view.

We sat back and enjoyed the drive.

Bumped on to a curb and I did a sort of swerve of my nerves at the view exposed to cliché blacks' men hammering up flasks on Ellis' door matt.

We swayed out the car and one of them noticed,

he started clapping in an exceeding way and exclaimed. "you damn right heroic due, that cop was on my ass for robbing a mother fucking Pepsi, you saved me, thank the lord."

there was a laughter from us and the dazzling crowd.

We stepped across them through the door and into the score, the surprise, the surprise.

We walked up the stairs with our eyes bleared and awed. My mouth was dry like the ice outside.

The apartment to which he owned smelt of home, that was the tame side.

"Who busted the door open? I asked. Ellis was already warmed for a fight.

We seeped into the abode. Peered into a sight, a picture. There was a purr.

Part 2 - Chapter 3

A cat peered over the chair and Ellis had tears in his eyes.

Berry laid down like a rug she was thrown on. A red bleach was sinking into her blue dress, like an alarm gun.

What looked to me as a thousand scars was in her chest. We looked at each in shock. His fist hit the ground with a thud and the wooden plank it hit broke.

"Don't blame yourself…" I spoke over the disaster. A silence loomed with the resonance of dystopic anger.

He turned to me, his eyes now a waterfall, he sprawled over it kit her goodbye. He pounced up with crimson stains over his striped red t shirt – you could tell the difference.

"I'll find who did this, just a matter of time, check for any indication of identity in this place."

I, questioning, "what's the cat for?"

"part of the surprise, I guess. It's yours."

"Imma call it Pooch."

"...Hot dang..."
We clued over the scene, found a grey bandana, and a torn knackered navy cloth, from a coat we both assumed.
"Right,' exclaimed Ellis, "looks to me like Mexican with a fashion sense came in here and used her like piñatas. There's that chino wearing fellow down on henry drive. Let's take a drive down there, pop some heads up for some answers."

I grabbed pooch, Ellis: The L&B.

The black crowd had left the porch leaving

matches and beer cans, some red stripe I recall.

Put pooch in the back of the car, glanced at the bullet hole in the cars, hopped in passenger seat and waited for Ellis to finish his cigarette. He looked like he was planning. It was gloomy. Pooch purred, Ellis flicked his cig and swung into driver's seat and punched in gear.

He was swerving and turning the streets in a discrete cruise, clearly hurt.

"It's alright, no cop gonna stop at this hour." I claimed.

"Darn tootin,' he proclaimed

We pulled up on henry street, a kinda Hispanic local, out on the outskirts of town. We didn't know any Mexicans, so we drove by asking some sort of head honcho. Tok till the third guy before we got answers. He was a skinny man, maybe a teen, wore a ripped denim jacket and chinos. (as we expected).

"hey who's the head honcho round here, the taco provider?" Ellis nobly remarked.

The guy turned his head, said, "gringos, ey, hey hey I know who to speak to.'

"You for real?" Ellis asked

"Hombre my cousin Paul can get you anything you need, what you looking for?"

"Esse, we need some damn answers quick," I talked with a raised voice.

"Well heck let me hop in, I'm going to his anyway.

"Jump in,'" Ellis replied with an elusive stare at the dashboard.

He directed us to a pristine bungalow, a small

house lit with every kind of colour, looked like a rainbow this time of night. We hopped out and the skinny fella shouted: "Paul! My cousin, company, ey, ey."

Part 2 - Chapter 4

Paul entered the yard, jeans and a tank top wearing a sombrero.

Ellis and I took a look at each other and approached the house, the lad from the street was called Joe – we found that out on the ride.

"These two want some answers." Joe stated.

"You two want some weed?" asked Paul.

"Yeah we do." Ellis winked.

Damn we were in it. "Come on in." Paul offered.

He sat us down on the suede yellow sofa, a picture of a lily, the room was kinda ashy orange, filled with treys and cereal boxes.

"So, what do you want, huh?" inquired Paul.

"My girlfriend, Berry, we been looking to smack who killed her." revealed Ellis.

"Damn son that's a pretty name." Paul hospitably spoke.

"Her face was pretty; we found a grey bandana and a piece of cloth. Have a looksie." Ellis put them in Pauls hands.

Paul examined in puzzled intuition... He felt them as if they were a pair of tits and handed them back.

"They take any money?"

"No." replied Ellis.

"Well it weren't no junkie, this bandana looks familiar and this blue is part of a fed uniform, damn, and I know who's this grey piece of thrash belongs to."

We sat in patience

"That fucker PC Cowboy, you seen him?"

We both shook our heads, then lapsed back into inquisition.

Paul began to speak in a swing, "see this cop, dirtier than a hobo, runs bail for the quintiinos, Italian thugs. He releases them when they get nicked. Bring confiscated drugs back to them. But the thing is, he's a real golfer, dim as a broken bulb. Wears this bandana on the range. Wants pepple to know he has a gun, and he'd shoot it quicker than his dick. He lives just across the street."

"No problem." I replied, Ellis darted to the window. Looked at an antique house, a mash of flower and figurines of horses.
A skull above the porch.

Joe jumped in, "you gonna need `any guns, we

can help you with this resignation. He haw."

Ellis turned back to me, "how should we go about this, Aaron? He's right there sleeping on his yard with a beer can, in his pyjamas."

"We should tie him up and then give him something to wake him up." I retorted.

"You got any rope?" asked Ellis.

Paul blurted out, with no hesitation, a "yup." went to the garage with rope and pepper spray.
"This is for the hogtie.," he threw the rope, "I'll keep the spray her for his alarm." he put the pepper spray on the glass table, that had the words: 'can you see me.' written in some felt pen and a beer.

Ellis ventured on to the street and on to the cop's domain in an ordered scuffle. Passed the duck statue and on to the white porch.

Looked over, grabbed him, took him over the street to Pauls, whispering, he's heavier than a few dun bells.

We got in the house, roped his arms and legs and put him on the faint floor.

Part 2 - Chapter 5

[Paul began to roll a joint]

Joe commenced, "say, who wants to spray him like a wall?"

"I will." Ellis took the can with a pale hand, Paul flipped the rizla

Joe butted in, "can we have some music."

I shook my head.

Paul sparked the joint.

There was a hiss from the pepper spray, a sizzling joint.

Then a wail, wail, from cowboy. His eyes turned bloody with tears cascading out his face.

Cowboy spat and shouted "fuck you! I'm gonna gut ya." Ellis slapped him silly.

Paul passed the spliff to Joe.

"Why did you kill her?!" Ellis demanded.

"You know why. Killing Mr Jefferson. He ran the show, payback. Slap me once Mo"

Fwap. A cold blow to the grin on his chin. And another, another.

Joe passed me the joint.

The punches rolled like a bowling ball in an ecstatic vapid succession. Till his fists were bold with bruises.

Cowboy laughed.

I took a stance and reached back with my leg and kicked.

A burst of blood slashed out of his mouth, his head hit back, and joe smiled.

I passed the joint to Ellis.

"I got a plan for the both of you. Take him out on to the rail roads, the tracks and end him. There. Put this bandana on him too." suggested Paul

"That's a great plan." remarked Ellis.

"And do it soon. Whilst it's still dark."

"Can do," we duoed.

Ellis toked calmly, (with aggression).

"Let's go." Ellis insisted. "I picked the body up. Put him in the boot of the car whilst Ellis thanked our hombres. "have a safe day, thanks guys."

Ellis flicked the joint on to the concrete street, entered the car with a silent breath.

Part 2 - Chapter 6

The trunk was screaming a seemingly sarcastic rant about a showdown. They'd find him in the morning.

"Rawhide." I sang in tune with the radio. The back bucket growled with a moan. Ellis was in latitudes, thinking of a ship that could take us and rip away from a malignant existence.
I stared at him.
This is it…
The light son over the hill; we were there. The railroad and all of its divisions of its rust refurbishment. Congruent stone and tin; with a wailing whack, knocked him flat on his back and hit him, on the sunny side.

Cowboy Spit

"Bandits huh," he paused, there was a train raking rattle, "damn you gonna hit the bank."

We sternly took our backs and walked up the hill. And all was swill and swell.

Pouch placed his paw on my hands. There was half a second of shouting. Then splat, it got the twat, blood dashed dust over the vista, with our nodding heads. Under the circumstance we felt angelic, pouch unified with us y purring and placing his paw on my hand.

We bludgeoned our way through breakfast, flashed home to ring the police.

The officer that arrived to address Berry's body talked in a beguiled way, flashing words about like a fiesta, and custom; 'apologies'. The limerick of the officer's flourish was nourished in sugar. He had a hot chocolate. It was nearing 12. we basically plated Berry's body out of the house and to the morgue.

The officer left, we didn't know if he knew, he was actually really pleasant. We didn't know if he was on pay roll. He told us he was called jimmy. We pondered our lifestyle.

Part 2 - Chapter 7

A paw and a purr and I was in the dive.
Summer set in the morning a bird was tooting and, in a moment,, I could suck it clean. But would the morn awaken from dusk in a rapid musk. I am on my way. That is the muse, vampire shoes. There I was at the racetracks, on prowl for blood, a policeman as such, I ate him up. It'll be a funny day I know. The rabbit ran as the case of dogs wrapped round the circuit. And one dog got a trophy. I took his neck and knew not to spill. 'he'll be dry soon; I'll eat his brains with a spoon... '

Three men entered, damn they caught me, for I am not a dog and there is no mourning. I jumped out the window.

Part 2 - Chapter 8

I woke up with pooch on my chest, a bright yawn, and a bullet in my leg. Ellis called me Peggy. I had been dreaming of pooch and had a sore day. We ate cereal and pancakes, ate them up like sniffing snuff, puff, puff. I was shot the night before and was still in a misty haze.

Just after jimmy left, /we went and bought some suits early in the morning, got Pooch some food and had a sandwich. Oh, what a bright day. We headed off wearing the spic and span that was a two-piece, man, all along the day. Smoked up, flipped up and pissed up; we sauntered down a neat street, a red car passed by.

We talked of the remedy, other frequencies, in a handsome gesture. To which was our liberty (we demanded). At a glance we noticed the camera store and knew what needed to happen.

We sought to purchase something nice and tidy.

In stride, we were becoming vigilantes, booming down the avenue.

We followed round an Italian in a suit till he was greeted by a police officer in a back street who pulled out a bag, Ellis took a picture, but the flash went off.

One of the Quintinos shot at us for taking pictures of a drug deal, the pc got off quicker than a wasp.

We were shouting reason, that we wanted justice.

It was a whole hang do of a fiasco. He told us to come out with our hands up.

The Italian started speaking, "you want to take down crime?"

"No" I reprimanded, "we want the police force to be cleaned up."

"As it happens, we are in need of you two, we want to just have a militia, so things get done easily, help our operation's run smoothly. do you think you could rally some men and take down the police force?" the Italian was telling us what we needed to hear.

He gave us some guns. We stashed them in the car.

Part 2 - Chapter 9

Pancakes with a melodious vibe and a nice indicating of a new horizon. It was bonny with sun.

Ellis stated, "in all ways a good day."

A pop smashed the window and a swat force stimulated outside, we dove out the back of Ellis' apartment; falling down to the ground, shots were fired at us, and in a away we were to toil through the car boot. We drew out a rifle and a handgun, as so in must we sprang round to see a swat member and shot him in the chest, and he was dead.

Along the northern front of town, a gang had started rising and rioting, with the sound of shooting escalating from the town hall.

There was the verge of anarchy looming. thuds and punches. We saw a force emerge on the other side of the policemen.

I yelled, "jimmy!"

A voice recoiled back; "yeh!"

"Stand down," I implied.

"Make us." he replied

"Let us see the mayor." Ellis suggested.

"What for?" Jimmy was puzzled.

"Make our militia legal, all you cops do is kill people who make noise. And the people run the town." I stated.

"fine, we'll get him out, but our murder rate has gone down," a joke Jimmy jumped to.

The mayor leaped out like a hare, with some paper and *pen*.

We struck a peace accord, and the militia became the ruling force of the town. That we would take on responsibility of new canter. We raised an old flag from the town hall, just a black and white skull print. Had a pint with Ellis, smoked, and the sky was gleaming with sun shining off the ice snow. We went back to Ellis apartment. "on the way we are at last.," remarkably, "all is hunky dory." to the car and down the drying road, we were home, fumed with l&b cigs. In brewing haste towards another beer from the fridge. A sip and slip into a trance, beer being so assuring.

There was a filling silence.

Ellis started speaking: "I think we should do something for Berry, like graffiti, it was her hobby, she showed me tricks, we have to do a ceremony." some facts hard lain.

I grabbed pouch, Ellis; the keys, and drove around looking for grand wall. Everything had a peaceful renascence, I heard a whistle and the rain began to pour, we dove in to bar, the slappin' shots emerged. Vodka and whiskey. We hit the glasses together hard on top, then comes along guy with dreadlocks.

We played a few rounds of shots till, the Afro Caribbean fell like a rock on the bar floor, Ellis lifted him into a taxi, Bob Marley shuffled on the jukebox

Part 2 - Chapter 10

Then immediately a woman in scarlet stocking, crimson lip stick black skinny shorts, and velvet hair, eyes were blue, her top willowy white; with blonde hair frazzled by rain. I had to watch the walk, I had dire means to have her. went with a sway to her side, see if we could talk.

Ordered two doubles, she started smiling: a kinda campfire glow of the face.

We began to move close together, when she grabbed my hand and lead me upstairs, where we had ups and downs. Sex, so to say.

Whilst Ellis ordered a triple gin, lime slice, and did the karaoke.
I was pursing nickers and putting my jeans back on when she goes, "I'm FBI, put em up."

I moved around the bed, struck a look at her, threw my top over her head. Then with a shuffling rustle, her head hit the wall and she was out clean.

I got dressed, grabbed the gun, put a coat on the woman, then picked her up and took her downstairs, a scene dazzled by scotch bourbon and a few lagers were being tossed about. Ellis saw the sight and ran over, he plunged through her coat belongings only to find an FBI badge, Agent Waller. The gang had assembled round the ruby sofa she was lain on, next to the bar.

A bust in and pub and grub.

Part 2- Chapter 11

She started waking up, one eye after another, she tried to get up, but she was put back done when she started talking: "look, I'm just her on a mission to find a serial killer.

A real who done it.

"A serial killer, ey." Ellis asked.

She started speaking, "there was a killing down south, two people victimised. The killer leaves a lily as a calling card. I followed his trail to new canter. As soon as I arrived to here, I was informed of a murder at the farm on the edge of town."

Ellis and I glanced at each other, I questioned "so you want help?" there was a glimpse at the manic future.

"You bet ya."

A silence loomed over for a few minutes.

I helped the agent up and we inquired, "will you leave our militia alone if we catch the killer, if we get him alive, we want some gold as well?"

"Sure, if we catch him alive." she answered.

Ellis stated, "the devils shit storm will be done by morning."

"Ellis, I'm gonna go alone on this one." I spoke.

"Then I'll take pooch, light a candle, get some spray paint; meet me at brush bank wall." Ellis noted, it was 3pm.

I asked Waller her name, she told me it was Tracy. Tracy Waller.

Ellis ordered a whiskey at the bar. From there we separated. I suggested we head to the town florist, she agreed. We arrived at the shop but there was a sign saying, 'back in 5'. we started observing the flowers, smoking cigs. She gave a flirt my way, and I gave her a kiss; seconds before the florist showed up., we offered a hello to him. We gracefully asked, "do you sell dark Lilly's?"

"Yes, I do. Why do you want some?"

"We're looking for someone who bought these Lilly's." she stated.

"Well, a bloke about yey big came in here, his big head and a baseball bat, yellow t shirt."

"Name?' I asked

"I call him the Bahamas butcher; said if I didn't give him those Lilly's he'll bash my skull in. Eat me uplike shrimp on a stick. Thought to oblige him."

"Damn, hooey, you done missed a missile." I stated, Waller vibrated.

"Know where he is?" asked Waller.

"He was on a Harley Davison, said he was gonna go fishing, the only place to do that is the lake." the florist suggested.

"We'll go find out, thanks for the lead."

We got a taxi up there, to the only cabin near the shore. A hard man figure of a log construction, which smelt of beer, bile and bone broke through the door

"Who the hell are you?" He figured shouted.

"Are you the Bahamas butcher?" I had to shouted back.

"Well I must damn be, damn celebrity. You want my autograph."

He was naked of course. he began to run with the bat, swept at me. I snooped left and swung up with an uppercut, few jabs, then a kick; he clambered to the floor: a K.O.

"Where's your part of the deal, Tracy?"

"I'll get a helicopter down here, then you can have some gold."

We waited with rump, both our chests locked together, with snuzzling and a brief cuddling in the log cabin, next to a lake sunset.

The helicopter landed and out of the passenger seat a man in black emerged.

"Hoffter."

"Agent Waller."

"We have completed the mission, sir. In

exchange for help, we have to give this man some gold, and for his town to be run by a militia with no interference." She demanded.

"Yes, you brought him back alive thanks chap." Hoffter agreed.

"I'll radio in."

"Whiskey, Bronco, Gary, Golf, Gecko, Piccadilly, requisition for gold from Agent Hoffter."

"Confirmed. We will tell the bank to relinquish some gold to you, here's a check." he walked back to the copper turned around and went, "you won't be interfered with." and put his shades on.

The other armed FBI members grabbed the culprit, putting him into custody.

"I'll ride that bike back to town. You can go now, love in peace."

We kissed and there was a bliss in her eyes like Twinkling stars. The hug stopped and she left for the helicopter. I the motorbike, keys were already in.

I slapped to town; speed of the breeze put me in ease. When I got to the wall Ellis spoke of.

A colourful art had overcome the difficult dark, black, wall. With white flowers, fruit growing on stems – purple (ripe). In blue: 'Berry' was written.

"She was already an angel." Ellis grieved and, the smoke from his cig was dandy.

"I know buddy, we have to go into town. I have a cheque for some gold."

"That sounds great."

"Now we run the town, let's do a festival."

"Rock and roll, eh"

"We'll go into town to the bank and arrange for it to be set up and save some gold for the future the town."

Ellis showed a look I'd never seen before, "everything is fine." his words formed lovingly.

Part 2 - Chapter 12

We awoke the next day with a kinky knock on the door, hung over and delirious, we woke and legged to the door in stupor.

Waft the door swung open, a crack on the door mat, it was Blakely, "everything alright chaps, I'm back from my trip." He was our old friend, we hung out all the time, since he went on holiday.

I asked, "how, why, damn it's a pleasure to see you again we thought you were fish food by now. And you're wearing a suit. Like us."

"Good to see you man." Ellis remarked "big cock and balls is back. While you were gone, we got a bunch of gold. Let us go to the bank. Simples"

The three of us left pooch snoring, and got the permit for a performance, went to big Bronco Billy to arrange some bands to come to town, he gestured, " we want the rock on, a jam that never stops." Ellis spoke.

The stage was put up and the town was in a relished ruckus, we thought let's kick back and have a fun one.

It took a few days to arrange all the band. in a week it was ready.

We waited; wafting L&B smoke out the window. There was a beautiful bashing of positivity, beating of the chest. It was time to hear the mash blast pass the past.

A stupendous show of rapid rock memorised the crowd sounding like love and trust. The stage was a shadow of black, a banner. Red rock. The bands rolled their music in beauty.

The audience stood strong, with the splashing of lights, reds, and blues. And twangs that rang round like a boomerang. A hammering of notes hitting a crescendo sweet and mood leaking through as the rifts shifted, a greasy vibe to the strings stride.

Greatness was taking place as a wicked, grizzly bands sang of peace.

The festival groomed three days to be happy with a cascade joy.

On the third day, at midnight, it ended, the three of us and pooch started at the moon light, as the ramming of noise reverberated through our minds. We convulsed beers as pooch nodded to sleep.

We shuffled a few games of cards, Blakley won mostly.

The table started filling with beer bottles.

Till we all honked out early in the morn.

The morning was quiet, but we were all cajoled in energy, there was a hippy eccentricity to folk we walked pass to get breakfast. Seemed like a marvellous movement passed by. With the liqueur loose, tail too. Happiness flew to the suns tune.

Printed in Great Britain
by Amazon